# Meet the Schoolies

**Mrs. Meow**
Best teacher in school

**Larry Einstein**
Always has a bright idea

**Kitty**
Loves nature and pink

**Hayden Hoot**
School math whizz

**Leeza Ladybug**
Loves drama class

**Newman Beaker**
Science project genius

**Spencer**
Fastest owl in school

**Suzy Snail**
Great at spelling

**Chip**
Enjoys singing a lot

**Lydia Ladybug**
Loves music class

**Sid Snail**
Top of the class

**Pete Hopper**
Loves colors

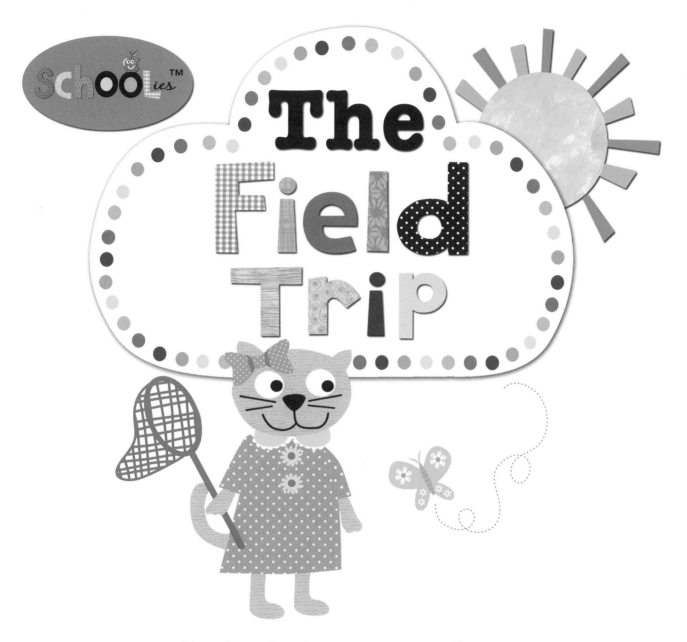

# Schoolies™

# The Field Trip

Based on the characters created by
**Ellen Crimi-Trent**

priddy books

Today was a special day.
The Schoolies were going on a
field trip to the Nature Center!

The Schoolies had brought paper and pencils.

They were all going to make maps
as they walked along the nature trail.

Soon they arrived at the Nature Center, and visited the pond.

At the water's edge, Spencer stuck his feet in the mud.

Butterflies

Kitty really wanted to see the butterflies.

In the butterfly garden, Kitty waited
for the butterflies to come.
She was very quiet.

Kitty was too busy
looking for butterflies,
she didn't notice
Mrs. Meow leading
the Schoolies away.

Mrs. Meow led the Schoolies into the woods.
She showed them different kinds of trees.

The Schoolies came to a giant tree.

How many Schoolies will it take to make a ring around this tree?

The Schoolies ran back to the cave.

Kitty isn't in the cave.

...and through
the woods...

Kitty told the Schoolies how she'd been left behind.

On the way home,
Larry gave Kitty his map.